She and Sebastian were twins, and they loved each other very much.

"I saw him when the storm was at its very worst," replied the captain, "The mast had broken off and he was clinging to it. If he held on for long enough, he might have survived."

Then there is hope, thought Viola. She knew she would cry if she kept thinking about her brother, so she changed the subject. "What country is this?" she asked.

"This is Illyria," said the captain. "I was born here! You see that great palace over there? That's where Duke Orsino lives.

He's the ruler here; he's a good man. And that big house over there? That's the home of the Countess Olivia. Poor soul, she's so sad: her brother's just died."

The moment the words were spoken, the captain knew he'd said the wrong thing.

"I-I-I'm sorry, my lady," he stammered. "I didn't mean..."

"It's all right," said Viola.

"And I'm sure a great lady such as yourself would receive a warm welcome in either place," the captain went on.

"I'm too upset to be a guest anywhere," said Viola, shaking her head. "If people knew about the shipwreck and my poor lost brother, they'd make such a fuss. I can't bear the thought of that.

Tales from Shakespeare

Twelfth Night

Antonio
Sebastian's friend, a sailor

Sir Toby Belch
Olivia's uncle

Viola
a young woman, later
disguised as a man
called Cesario

Sebastian
Viola's twin brother

Malvolio
Olivia's steward

Feste
Olivia's jester

Sir Andrew
Aguecheek
Sir Toby's friend

Orsino
Duke of Illyria

Olivia
a countess

Maria
Olivia's housekeeper

Timothy Knapman

Illustrated by Yaniv Shimony

Shipwreck and Heartbreak

Act one

What country, friends, is this?
– Viola

Viola stood on the beach and looked out at the calm sea. She could hardly believe that just hours ago her ship had been smashed to pieces by a storm. Its broken remains now lay scattered across the sands around her.

It was only by chance that she had survived. The ship's captain had found her and dragged her to shore.

"Was there any sign of my brother, Sebastian?" she asked the captain anxiously.

If only I could be someone else and forget my sadness for a while... That's it! I'll disguise myself as a young man and get a job at Duke Orsino's palace. Then, when I'm ready, I will tell everyone my real name!" Viola and the captain were happy with her plan.

Duke Orsino was miserable. He'd fallen head over heels in love with the beautiful Countess Olivia. But every time he sent a servant to tell her so, they brought back the same answer: Olivia was in mourning for her brother, and she didn't want to hear about love, not from anyone. Orsino didn't know what to do. He just sat around in despair, while his servants played sad music to him.

One day a handsome young man called Cesario came to the palace, asking for a job. Orsino took one look at him and had a brilliant idea.

"All the servants I've sent to Olivia have been old and ugly," he said to himself. "That's not very romantic! No wonder she turned them away. But if I send this handsome young man instead, she's much more likely to listen to him."

She will attend it better in thy youth
– Orsino

Orsino was suddenly full of energy and hope again. He wrote a brand new love letter to Olivia and asked Cesario to deliver it straight away.

"Of course, sir," said Cesario.

But the young man Cesario was hiding two things from Duke Orsino...

The first was that "he" was the lady Viola disguised as a boy; the second was that Viola had fallen in love with Orsino the moment she saw him.

As she walked to Olivia's great house, Viola was nervous. Orsino had been taken in by her disguise, but would it fool anyone else?

The door to Olivia's house was opened by her steward, Malvolio. He was strict and stern and didn't like to see anyone having fun. Malvolio looked Viola up and down as if there was a nasty smell under his nose.

"Not another message from the Duke Orsino?" he sneered. "My lady won't see you, boy."

Viola breathed a sigh of relief. "Then I will stay here until she does," she said.

Malvolio tried to make Viola leave, but she wouldn't budge. At last, he went and told Olivia there was a message for her.

"Very well then," Olivia sighed. "Let's give Orsino one last chance."

She put on her black veil and told Malvolio to show Orsino's servant in. Olivia read the letter; it was just like all the others Orsino had written: full of flowery phrases that sounded pretty but didn't really mean very much.

"Tell me, young man," said Olivia, "is this what you would say to a woman if you were in love with her?"

"I don't know," said Viola. "I've never been in love with a woman. But if you show me your face, perhaps I can try to imagine."

Olivia liked the look of this new servant of Orsino's, so she lifted her veil.

Viola could see that Olivia was very beautiful. She thought about what she would like a man to say to her if she was in love.

"Well I wouldn't send someone else to tell you I loved you," Viola said. "I'd come myself. And I wouldn't go away again, not ever.

Write loyal cantons of contemned love, And sing them loud even in the dead of night
    – Viola

I would write you poems and sing to you; I would make sure that you knew I loved you."

"You speak very well for a servant," said Olivia.

"I am from a good family," said Viola, "but I've had some bad luck."

Olivia thought a moment, and then she said, "Tell Orsino that I cannot love him, and I don't want to hear from him again. Unless... Unless *you* come back to tell me how he takes the news."

Viola bowed and left the room. She wondered what Olivia meant. She didn't realize that Olivia had just fallen in love with her, disguised as Cesario!

Making Mischief

Act two

Orsino wasn't the only person who wanted to marry Olivia. When Olivia's uncle, Sir Toby Belch, came to stay with her, he brought a friend with him.

Olivia's housekeeper opened the door to let them in.

"Maria, my darling!" said Sir Toby, giving her a big kiss. "Allow me to present Sir Andrew Aguecheek!"

Where Sir Toby was fat and red-faced, Sir Andrew was thin and pale. He took off his hat and bowed to Maria.

"Sir Andrew's a handsome devil, isn't he?" said Sir Toby.

Maria could see that he wasn't.

"And he's very clever," said Sir Toby.

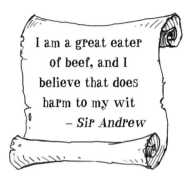

I am a great eater of beef, and I believe that does harm to my wit
– Sir Andrew

Maria could see that he wasn't.

"My niece Olivia will fall in love with him at first sight!" said Sir Toby.

Maria could see that she wouldn't. Olivia was beautiful and clever and Sir Andrew didn't stand a chance.

"You old rogue!" she said to Sir Toby. "You mean you've run out of money again and you're telling lies to this poor devil so that he'll keep buying you wine!"

"Wine?" said Sir Toby. "What an excellent idea! I'd love some." And he pushed past Maria and into the house.

Sir Toby and Sir Andrew stayed up late that night drinking. Feste, Olivia's jester, found them surrounded by empty bottles.

"My dear fellow!" Sir Toby bellowed at Feste. "I was wondering what had happened to you."

"Countess Olivia didn't want to hear my jokes after her brother died," said Feste sadly.

"Well we do," said Sir Toby, "but first, sing us a song."

Feste had a lovely voice, but it was soon drowned out when Sir Toby and Sir Andrew joined in. They made such a dreadful noise that Maria rushed into the room in her nightclothes.

"What time do you call this?" she cried. "Be quiet, you lot, or that bossy Malvolio will be down to tell you off!"

It was too late. There was Malvolio, standing in the doorway, looking furious.

"Masters, are you mad?" he said. "You should be ashamed of yourselves!"

"Just because you're a goody-goody, it doesn't mean the rest of us can't enjoy ourselves!" said Sir Toby.

"I have talked to my mistress about your bad behaviour and your... friend," Malvolio went on, looking at Sir Andrew with contempt. "And we have decided that if you can't behave yourselves, you'll have to leave this house!"

Is there no respect of place, persons, nor time in you?
– Malvolio

"Don't be so harsh Malvolio," said Maria. "They were just having a little party – they meant no harm. Please don't tell Olivia."

"If you had any respect for our mistress," said Malvolio, "you would have thrown these... *gentlemen* out yourself!" And with that he left.

"That pompous fool!" said Maria. "He acts as if it's his house, not Olivia's! How dare he tell me what I should do? I'll show him."

So crammed (as he thinks) with excellencies, that it is his grounds of faith that all that look on him love him
        – Maria

"What are you going to do?" asked Sir Toby.

"I'm going to write him a love letter of course!" said Maria. "He's convinced the whole world is in love with him. I'll show him how wrong he is!"

Meanwhile, Olivia's answer hadn't made Orsino any happier. Viola couldn't bear to see the man she loved looking so sad.

"Have you ever thought that there is a woman out there who loves you just as much as you love Olivia?" she said.

"Women can't love as deeply as men," said Orsino.

"Oh but they can," said Viola. "Men make more fuss about it, that's all. My father had a daughter who was in love with a man, and she felt just as much for the man she loved as you feel for Olivia."

"What happened to her?" said Orsino.

Viola so wanted to tell him the truth but she didn't dare.

"She never told the man," she said, "and her secret ate away at her."

"Did she die of a broken heart?" asked Orsino.

"I am the only daughter my father ever had," said Viola.

She never told her love, but let concealment, like a worm in the bud, feed upon her damask cheek
        – Viola

At once she knew that she had said too much, so she quickly added, "I mean, I am the only son!" And then she remembered her poor brother Sebastian, and she ran from the room in tears.

> I am all the daughters of my father's house, and all the brothers too
> – *Viola*

Maria had done what she had promised: she'd written Malvolio a love letter, but had made it look like it was written by Olivia.

That would teach Malvolio a lesson!

She put the letter on a bench in a part of the garden where Malvolio liked to walk. Then she, Sir Toby and Sir Andrew hid and waited. When Malvolio appeared, he was talking to himself.

"I know Olivia is much grander than me," he said, "but mistresses have married their servants in the past. I could be Count Malvolio and tell that Sir Toby to get lost!"

"Cheeky devil!" said Sir Toby.

"*Shush!*" whispered Maria. "He's seen the letter!"

"It looks like Olivia's writing," said Malvolio, picking the letter up. "What does it say? *I am in love with M.* Who can she mean? Wait a moment! My name begins with 'M'! She's in love with me!

"*I know you're not as important as I am, but that doesn't matter: people can become important. If you love me too, wear bright yellow stockings with black cross garters next time I see you.*

Some 'men' are born great, some achieve greatness, and some have greatness thrust upon them
      – The letter

And smile – you have such a lovely smile – that way I will know our love is true!"

Malvolio ran off, clutching the letter and scarcely able to contain his excitement.

Maria, Sir Toby and Sir Andrew tumbled out of their hiding place laughing.

"I can't believe he fell for it!" said Sir Toby. "But why yellow stockings with black cross garters?"

"Because they are what Olivia hates most of all!" said Maria. "He's going to make a complete fool of himself in front of her – I can't wait to see it!"

Confusions

Act three

Your servant's
servant is your
servant, madam
– *Viola*

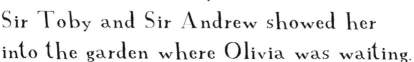

There was no sign of
Malvolio when Viola
arrived later that day. Instead,
Sir Toby and Sir Andrew showed her
into the garden where Olivia was waiting.

"I am Cesario," said Viola, "your servant."

"I remember you," said Olivia, "but you
are Orsino's servant, not mine."

"Orsino is in love with you," said
Viola, "so everything that is his belongs
to you."

"I am bored of hearing about Orsino,"
said Olivia. "I just want to hear about you."

Viola noticed that Olivia was blushing.

"Haven't you realized?" said Olivia.
"Don't you know that I love you, Cesario?"

Viola finally understood. Poor Olivia
had been completely taken in by Viola's
disguise and had fallen in love with her!

I have one heart, one bosom, and one truth, And that no woman has; nor never none Shall mistress be of it, save I alone.
— *Viola*

"I am sorry, my lady, but I have never loved a woman," said Viola.

She couldn't bear to see the sad look on Olivia's face, so she turned and walked away at once.

Sir Toby found Sir Andrew in his bedroom, packing his bags.

"What are you doing?" Sir Toby asked.

"I may be a fool," said Sir Andrew, "but I'm not an idiot! I saw how Olivia looked at that servant, Cesario. She's in love with him. I don't stand a chance, so I'm leaving!"

Sir Toby realized that if Sir Andrew left, there would be no one to buy him wine! He had to do something.

"Of course she *pretended* to like him," he said.

I saw your niece do more favours to the Count's serving-man than ever she bestowed upon me
— *Sir Andrew*

"She was trying to make you jealous!"

"Jealous?" said Sir Andrew.

"You know what women are like!" said Sir Toby. "They love it when men fight over them. Hey, that's not a bad idea! You should challenge Cesario to a duel. You're bound to beat him and then Olivia will have to marry you!"

"I am rather good in a fight," Sir Andrew said, drawing his sword and nearly poking himself in the eye. "Ouch! All right, I'll stay."

At that moment, Maria burst in. "Sir Andrew, Sir Toby! Come with me. I've just seen Malvolio – and he looks ridiculous!"

Not far away, two more shipwreck survivors had at last arrived in Illyria. One was a sailor called Antonio. The other was the young man whose life he'd saved: Viola's twin brother Sebastian.

The storm had carried them miles up the coast. On their journey to Illyria, they'd become good friends.

Sebastian wanted to see the famous sights of this beautiful place, but Antonio was wary. Long ago, he had fought against Duke Orsino in a great sea battle. Even today, he still had many enemies in Illyria.

I do not without danger walk these streets
– Antonio

"I'll wait for you at the Inn," Antonio told Sebastian. "You can come and join me once you've had a look around. Take care of yourself, my friend."

The two men embraced and then went their separate ways.

Olivia was searching through the rooms of her great house when she bumped into Maria.

"Where is Malvolio?" she asked. "He doesn't answer when I call for him and I want him to go and bring back that young man of Orsino's."

"Here he comes, my lady," said Maria.

She needed all of her strength not to burst out laughing when Malvolio appeared. Instead of his usual frown, he was smiling like an idiot. Instead of his usual black clothes, he was wearing bright yellow stockings with cross garters.

"There you are!" said Olivia. "I've been waiting for you!"

"I'm sure you have, my lady," said Malvolio, and he waggled his gartered legs in front of her.

"Are you quite all right, Malvolio?" said Olivia.

"I may not be as important as you," said Malvolio, "but people can become important. I read that not so long ago, didn't I, my lady?" and he winked at her.

"Is there something wrong with your eye?" said Olivia.

"No, my lady," said Malvolio, "just my heart." He waggled his legs again.

"I think Malvolio's gone mad," Olivia whispered to Maria.

Why appear you with this ridiculous boldness before my lady?
– Maria

This is very
midsummer
madness
– Olivia

"It looks that way," said Maria. "Leave him to us, my lady. We'll take care of him."

"Very well," said Olivia. As she left the room, Malvolio blew her a kiss.

"I think you'd better come with us, Malvolio," said Sir Toby soothingly.

"Don't touch me!" said Malvolio. "I'm better than the whole lot of you. You'll see what I mean soon enough!" And he ran out into the garden.

"Oh dear," said Maria, "I think this is getting out of hand. Sir Toby, you should go after him."

Viola was walking back to Orsino's palace when Malvolio ran past her, with Sir Toby and Sir Andrew chasing after him. When Sir Andrew caught sight of Viola, he ran into a tree.

"Ouch!" he said and he shook his head to clear it. "It's you! How dare you steal the woman I love!"

"What are you talking about?" said Viola.

"I demand a duel!" said Sir Andrew, taking out his sword and nearly poking himself in the eye again.

"I don't want to fight you," said Viola.

"I'm not surprised you don't," said Sir Toby, "because Sir Andrew here is the scariest swordfighter in the whole country!"

"You leave him alone!" said a voice.

"Pick on someone your own size!"

A man in sailor's clothes stepped out of the shadows and stood between Viola and Sir Andrew.

"I know you!" said Sir Toby and he drew his sword. "You're that villain Antonio, who fought against Orsino in the great sea battle! Hands up! I'm taking you to prison."

"Would somebody please tell me what is going on?" said Viola.

Antonio turned to her and said, "My dear friend, please help me!"

"I'll do anything I can," she said, "but I have no idea who you are."

"After everything we've been through?" said Antonio. "After I saved your life!"

"Forgive me," said Viola.

If this young gentleman have done offence, I take the fault on me
– Antonio

"But I don't know what you're talking about."

"You can't do this to me!" said Antonio.

"Come on, Sir Andrew," said Sir Toby. "Tie this rascal's hands. We're sure to get a reward for him."

"I'll deal with you later," said Sir Andrew to Viola, trying to put his sword back in his sheath and stabbing himself in the foot instead. "Ouch!"

Antonio took one last look at Viola before they took him off to jail.

"How could you do this, Sebastian?" he said.

Sebastian! Of course! Viola realized that Antonio had mistaken her for her twin brother – and that could mean only one thing: Sebastian was still alive!

Strange Meetings

Act four

"Feste!" said Olivia. "I think Malvolio has lost his mind. I was going to send him to fetch Cesario, but would you do it instead?"

"Of course, my lady," said Feste.

He went out into the town to look for the young man and finally found him wandering the streets like a tourist.

"There you are!" said Feste.

"I'm sorry," said the young man, "but I don't think we've met."

The young man was quite right, because he wasn't Viola at all, but her brother Sebastian! Sebastian looked so much like Viola that Feste couldn't tell the difference.

"Don't make jokes, Cesario," Feste said, "that's my job."

"I have no idea what you're talking about," said Sebastian. "Who is Cesario?"

"I'll go and get my lady Olivia," said Feste. "We'll see what she has to say about this."

"The poor fellow's not just a jester but a lunatic," said Sebastian to himself.

But no sooner had Feste gone, than Sebastian ran into Sir Toby and Sir Andrew.

"You again!" said Sir Andrew, drawing his sword and accidentally cutting his hand.

"Ouch!" said Sir Andrew.

"What now?" said Sebastian. "This whole country is full of lunatics!"

"Never mind that!" said Sir Andrew. "Fight me, you scoundrel!"

"All right then," said Sebastian, and he punched Sir Andrew on the nose.

"Ooh, that hurt!" said Sir Andrew.

"Stop this at once!" said a voice. It was Olivia! "Sir Toby, Sir Andrew, you should be ashamed of yourselves! Oh my poor Cesario, did they hurt you?"

"No," said Sebastian. Why did people keep calling him Cesario? He was beginning to think that maybe he was going mad.

I am mad, or else this is a dream
– Sebastian

34

"Will you forgive them?" said Olivia. "Will you come back to my house where I can take care of you?"

Sebastian looked at Olivia. She was the most beautiful woman he had ever seen and he fell in love with her on the spot.

"Yes please!" he said.

When Feste returned to the house, Maria asked him to go and see Malvolio in the darkened room where he was locked up.

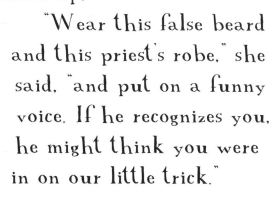

"Wear this false beard and this priest's robe," she said, "and put on a funny voice. If he recognizes you, he might think you were in on our little trick."

Malvolio hated people laughing and joking so he'd always been rude to Feste. Feste was determined to mock him while he had the chance.

"Is this where the lunatic lives?" he asked in a funny, old man's voice, as he peered in at Malvolio.

"Who's that?" Malvolio cried.

"I am Sir Topas the holy man," said Feste.

"Sir Topas, help me out of this darkened room, I beg you! I am not mad!" said Malvolio.

"Dark?" said Feste. "It isn't dark! Look at the big windows letting in all the sunshine. You must be mad if you can't see them!"

"What?" said Malvolio in a bewildered voice. "Don't make fun of me, please."

Feste chuckled to himself as he remembered every insult Malvolio had ever hurled at him. Then he felt someone tap him on the shoulder; it was Sir Toby.

"I'm teasing Malvolio," said Feste. "Do you want a go?"

"No," sighed Sir Toby. "My niece Olivia just told me off and I've changed my mind. Let the poor devil out of there, can't you?"

Feste peered into the darkened room. Malvolio looked so miserable. Feste nodded to Sir Toby: the joke wasn't funny anymore and suddenly seemed cruel.

There was never man so notoriously abused
– Malvolio

Sebastian thought he must be dreaming. Only a few hours ago, he had arrived in Illyria with nothing. Now he was in love with a rich, clever, beautiful woman who loved him just as much in return! He didn't think he could be any happier, and then Olivia asked him to marry her.

"I would love to," he said.

True Love

Act five

"**P**lease, my lord," said Viola to Orsino, "summon the sailor Antonio from prison. I think he has news of my brother, Sebastian."

"I will send some of my soldiers to fetch him," said Orsino. "They can meet us at Olivia's house. That's where we're going now."

"Why, my lord?" said Viola.

"I'm taking your advice, at long last," said Orsino. "Enough of sending messengers! I am going to tell Olivia I love her in person!"

Antonio and the soldiers guarding him were waiting outside Olivia's gates when Orsino and Viola arrived.

"Are you Antonio, who fought so savagely against my men in the great sea battle?" asked Orsino.

That most ingrateful boy there by your side
– Antonio

"I am," said Antonio boldly. "I wouldn't have come within a hundred miles of this place if it hadn't been for that young man there – the one who betrayed me!" Antonio jabbed a dirty finger in Viola's direction.

But before she could say anything, the gates swung open and Olivia walked through them.

> Here comes the Countess: now heaven walks on earth!
> – *Orsino*

"My love, at last!" said Orsino, and he spread out his arms to embrace her. Olivia ignored him and walked straight up to Viola.

"What are you doing out here, Cesario?" she said.

Viola looked across at Orsino. "I am where I always want to be," she replied. "With the person I love and admire most in the world: Duke Orsino."

Him I love more than I love these eyes, more than my life
— Viola

"How can you say that," said Olivia, "now that you're my husband?"

"Cesario, have you betrayed me as well?" roared Orsino.

"My lord, please believe me, I don't know what she's talking about!" said Viola.

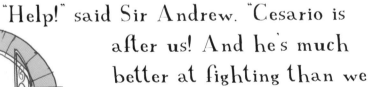

Again the gates clanged open. This time Sir Andrew and Sir Toby came limping through them, looking bruised and bloody.

"Help!" said Sir Andrew. "Cesario is after us! And he's much better at fighting than we are!"

Olivia and Orsino looked to Viola for an explanation, but she was bewildered too.

Then Sebastian came running through the gates!

"Olivia, my darling wife, there you are!" he said. "I am sorry that I hurt these men, but they kept on attacking me. Why is everyone looking at me?"

"The same face, the same voice... They must be the same person!" said Orsino, looking from Viola to Sebastian and back again.

"Antonio, my dear friend!" cried Sebastian. "What are you doing in chains? Here, let me help you out of them."

An apple cleft in two is not more twin than these two creatures.
– Antonio

"How can the same person be in two places at once?" said Antonio.

At last, Sebastian saw Viola.

"Who are you?" he asked Viola. "My father had no other sons, and yet we could be twins."

"We are," said Viola, "if you are the same Sebastian whose ship was wrecked in the storm. I am your sister Viola!"

"You're alive!" cried Sebastian. The twins burst into tears and hugged each other.

"At last I understand!" said Olivia, and Sebastian went over to her and kissed her.

"What a fool I've been!" said Orsino. "Olivia, I should congratulate you on your marriage."

"I'm sorry I couldn't love you, dear Orsino," said Olivia.

"Don't be sorry," Orsino replied.

"I think there's still a chance that my story will have a happy ending too. Viola – how odd it feels to call you by that name! – did you mean it just now when you said that you love me most in the world?"

"My lord," Viola replied, wiping tears of joy from her face, "I love you with all my heart."

"Then will you marry me, Viola?" said Orsino.

"I will!" said Viola.

I shall have share in this most happy wreck
— Orsino

"So here you all are!"

Everyone turned round. It was Malvolio. He was dirty and stooped from his time in the darkened room, but his eyes blazed with anger.

"See here, my lady?" he said, waving the letter at Olivia. "Does it not look like your handwriting? This is why I behaved so strangely to you."

"Maria wrote the letter," said Sir Toby, sheepishly. "I'm sorry, Malvolio."

"If you behave so badly to everyone," said Feste, "you can't blame them for getting their own back."

"Yes, I can!" spat Malvolio. "Just you wait!" He stormed off.

"Someone go after him," said Olivia. "The poor man has suffered so much."

Thus the whirligig of time brings in his revenges
– Feste

"At this happy time, I couldn't bear to think of anyone being miserable," said Orsino. "Viola, my love, let's go home. We have a wedding to plan – and everyone will be invited!"

The end

Consultant: Dr Tamsin Badcoe
Editors: Ruth Symons and Carly Madden
Designer: Andrew Crowson
QED Project Designer: Rachel Lawston
Editorial Director: Victoria Garrard
Art Director: Laura Roberts-Jensen

First published in the UK in 2015 by
QED Publishing
A Quarto Group company
The Old Brewery
6 Blundell Street
London N7 9BH

www.qed-publishing.co.uk

A catalogue record for this book is available from
the British Library.

ISBN 978 1 78493 003 5

Printed in China